This Walker
book belongs to:

This cake belongs to: ARONNY

This cake belongs to: Kievan

This cake belongs to:

Some things to know before you begin

Ronny Rock is about your age

Kieran is 14

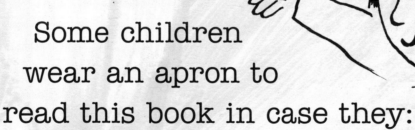

Some children wear an apron to read this book in case they:

a. dribble

b. read and eat messily at the same time

c. suddenly start making a cake

There's a quiz at the end, so pay attention to everything

For Shane and Sam MT • For Alvie, Ted and Ramona BI

First published 2011 by
Walker Books Ltd, 87 Vauxhall Walk,
London SE11 5HJ • 2 4 6 8 10 9 7 5 3 1 Text
© 2011 Merryn Threadgould • Illustrations ©
2011 Bruce Ingman • The right of Merryn Threadgould
and Bruce Ingman to be identified as author and illustrator
respectively of this work has been asserted by them in
accordance with the Copyright, Designs and Patents Act 1988 •
This book has been typeset in Franklin gothic and Baskerville •
Signatures by Sam Pomeroy and Finn McIver • Lettering and
mouse by Alvie Ingman • Printed in China • All rights reserved.
No part of this book may be reproduced, transmitted or stored
in an information retrieval system in any form or by any
means, graphic, electronic or mechanical, including
photocopying, taping and recording, without prior written
permission from the publisher • British Library
Cataloguing in Publication Data: a catalogue record for
this book is available from the British Library
ISBN 978-1-4063-3592-7 • www.walker.co.uk

RONNY ROCK starring in
MONSTER
CAKE MELTDOWN

Merryn Threadgould ● illustrated by Bruce Ingman

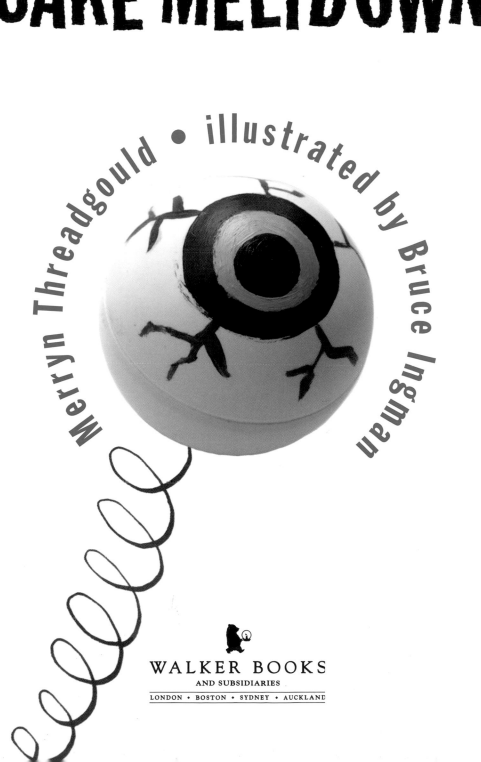

WALKER BOOKS

AND SUBSIDIARIES

LONDON · BOSTON · SYDNEY · AUCKLAND

Ronny Rock was a very lucky boy.

He didn't have loads of money or the latest computer games. At school he always got told off for talking in class, even if it wasn't him. And he was a bit rubbish at sport.

But he was very, very lucky. His friends thought so and Ronny thought so too.

Because Ronny lived with his dad.

And his dad owned a shop.

And that shop was the best shop in town, if not the WORLD.

It was on the High Street and had been there for ever. Above the window were three words:

ROCK THE BAKER

Rock the Baker was Ronny's dad.

To get into the shop you went through a wooden arch and then a door, which rang a little bell as you opened it.

ting-a-ling

Inside was a world so wonderful that some children got dizzy. Others laughed so much they had to be taken outside to calm down.

Everywhere you looked there were yummical things to eat. Tina, who worked in the shop, kept a cloth handy to wash drool off the glass display cabinets. And a bucket of water was kept near the door in order to revive people.

Every cake and loaf of bread in the shop was made by Mr Rock and his bakers and cooked in enormous ovens out the back.

Ronny Rock lived above the shop with his dad and he was allowed to choose a different cake every day for his lunch and for his tea, because Mr Rock thought cake was good for growing boys.

NOW can you see why Ronny was so very, very lucky?

1 cake for lunch +1 cake for tea = 2 cakes a day
2 cakes a day x 7 days a week = 14 cakes a week
14 cakes a week x 52 weeks a year = 728 cakes a year

Phew!

2 **Today was a Friday and on Fridays after school, Ronny was always in a hurry to get home.**

He zoomed out of St Cornstalks at record speed. He waited on the pavement for Stan Flan the lollipop man to stop the cars. Then he

took off and aeroplaned down the High Street. Two minutes and
ten seconds later he landed through the door of *Rock the Baker*. Tina
held out a doughnut, which he took as he taxi-ed past. He came to
a halt, with a mouthful of jam, in the bakery, where his dad was
decorating cakes.

Lots of children had their birthday parties on
Saturdays. So, Friday afternoons were spent
making birthday cakes and Ronny loved to help.

He found Mr Rock standing at a table with
a pile of plain cake on one side and a pile of
sweets and icing on the other.

"Ah, Captain Rock," said his dad. "Your flight's bang
on schedule. Read these birthday letters out to me and
help me work my magic." He handed Ronny a bunch of
cake request letters and flourished his icing knife like a
magician's wand. Ronny ate the last bit of doughnut and
read the first request.

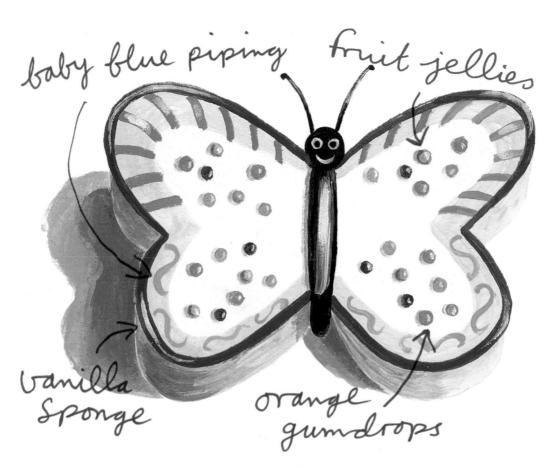

baby blue piping   fruit jellies

vanilla sponge

orange gumdrops

BEAUTIFUL BUTTERFLY

"Mildred Yeast, aged seven, wants a Beautiful Butterfly cake," said Ronny.

"Easy peasy lemon squeezy," said Mr Rock.

He cut out a butterfly shape from some of the cake and neatly covered it in pink and yellow icing. Then he got his piping bags and a box of nozzles and set about piping curls and swirls of colour and a smiling butterfly face. Very carefully, Ronny put fruit jelly spots on the wings. When it was finished, the cake looked like an expensive jewel.

"Nice," said Ronny.

"Next," said Mr Rock.

candy floss

chocolate icing

swiss roll

candied angelica

biscuit wheels

CHOCOLATE TRAIN

"Mrs Bloomer wants a Chocolate Train with candied angelica tracks," said Ronny.

Mr Rock got a swiss roll and covered it in smooth dark chocolate. He put candy floss steam coming out of a chocolate funnel. Then he cut strips of green angelica for the train tracks.

"What is angelica, dad?" asked Ronny.

"It's a kind of enormous prehistoric parsley boiled in sugar," replied Mr Rock. Ronny couldn't imagine any kid eating prehistoric parsley boiled in sugar.

"Next!"

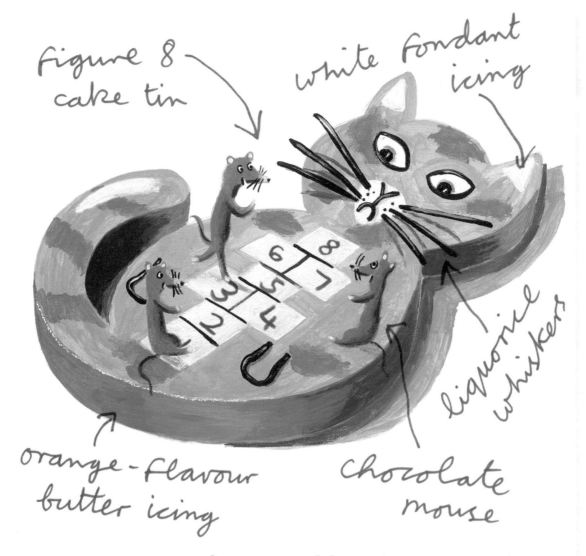

figure 8
cake tin

white fondant
icing

liquorice
whiskers

orange-flavour
butter icing

chocolate
mouse

Cat and Mice

"Sophie Barm wants a cake of some mice playing hopscotch on a cat." Ronny laughed. "Mice jumping on a cat! That's funny!"

"That's tricky!" said Mr Rock. "I'm off to the pictures at half past six. I hope I can get through these in time."

Once he finished the cat, who looked very cross with all the mice bouncing all over him, there was just one more cake to make.

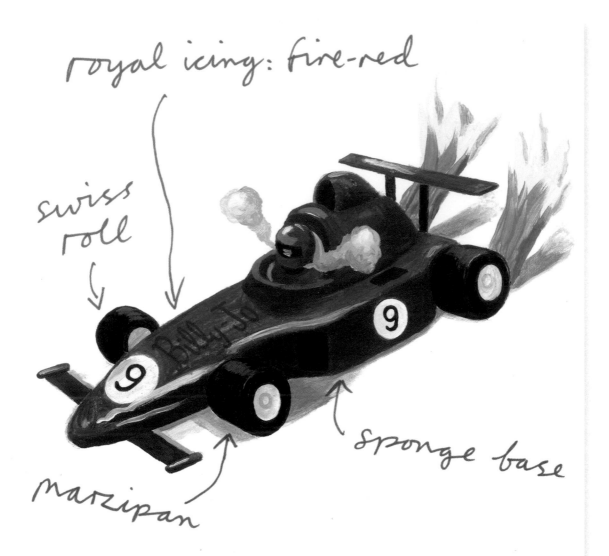

royal icing: fire-red

swiss roll

marzipan

sponge base

RACING CAR

"Billy Bran wants a Racing Car with its wheels on fire. Coooool!" said Ronny.

His dad said, "Kids these days have got too much imagination."

Mr Rock gave the racing car a shiny red body with hot orange flames shooting out of the wheels. Even though he was in a hurry, he added a driver with smoke coming out of his ears.

Ronny loved it. "That's the best one, Dad. You rock, Rock!" He gave his father a sticky high five. Ronny had invented this himself. You high five someone and then pretend your hands are stuck together.

By the time the birthday cakes were finished and everything was cleared up, it was half past six.

Mr Rock looked at his watch and said, "Where is that dratted boy?"

3 That dratted boy was Kieran, Ronny's childminder. His mum, Tina, worked in the shop. Kieran was 14 and looked after Ronny quite a lot. He was always late.

Mr Rock said he had less sense than a mealworm.

Kieran turned up, ten minutes late, moving in a very strange way. He liked to dress like an American rapper and his jeans were falling so far down he had to walk with bandy legs to keep them from falling right off.

Ronny thought he looked well cool.

"Oh, there you are," said Mr Rock. "And I can see why you are late. You had to get off your horse." He went off to the pictures, laughing at his own joke.

Kieran looked at Ronny and circled his finger round by his head, meaning, "Your dad's mental."

Ronny liked Kieran because they laughed at the same things. Kieran showed him how to burp the ABC, told him interesting stuff about girls and taught him how to play ping-pong. Kieran was the second best ping-pong player in his school.

Fig. 1. Player A gets on Player B's shoulders. Safety equipment must be worn.

Fig. 2. Player B launches bun.

Note: a stale bun is a batting bun.

Fig. 3. Vertical-pong.

Fig. 4. Tooth-pong – advanced.

Fig. 5. Follow-me-leader-pong.
Note: 1m min. distance between players.

1m

Fig. 6. Clearing Bun-pong arena.

Fig. 7. The lost letter – not part of normal play.

Once Mr Rock had definitely left the building, Kieran and Ronny played Bun-pong in the bakery, which they weren't allowed to do because they often broke things. To play Bun-pong, Ronny got on Kieran's shoulders, then Kieran threw a stale bun in the air and Ronny tried to hit it as hard as he could with one of Kieran's ping-pong bats.

After about half an hour, Ronny fell off Kieran's shoulders and the bun fell to bits. So Kieran started texting his mates and Ronny started picking up bits of bun to bung in the bin. The biggest bit of bun was lying near a flour sack. When Ronny bent down to get it, he saw a piece of paper poking out from under the sack. He picked it up. It was a lost cake request letter:

```
Dear Mr Rock,

I would like to order a birthday cake for
my son Alfie, aged four.
I will be in to collect it by ten on
Saturday, at the latest.
Thank you, and see you at ten on Saturday
(at the latest).
Yours, Mrs Mealman

P.S. Alfie would like a Monster Cake.
```

What a disaster!

It was Friday evening. Mr Rock was at the pictures. And Alfie Mealman's Monster Cake was not made.

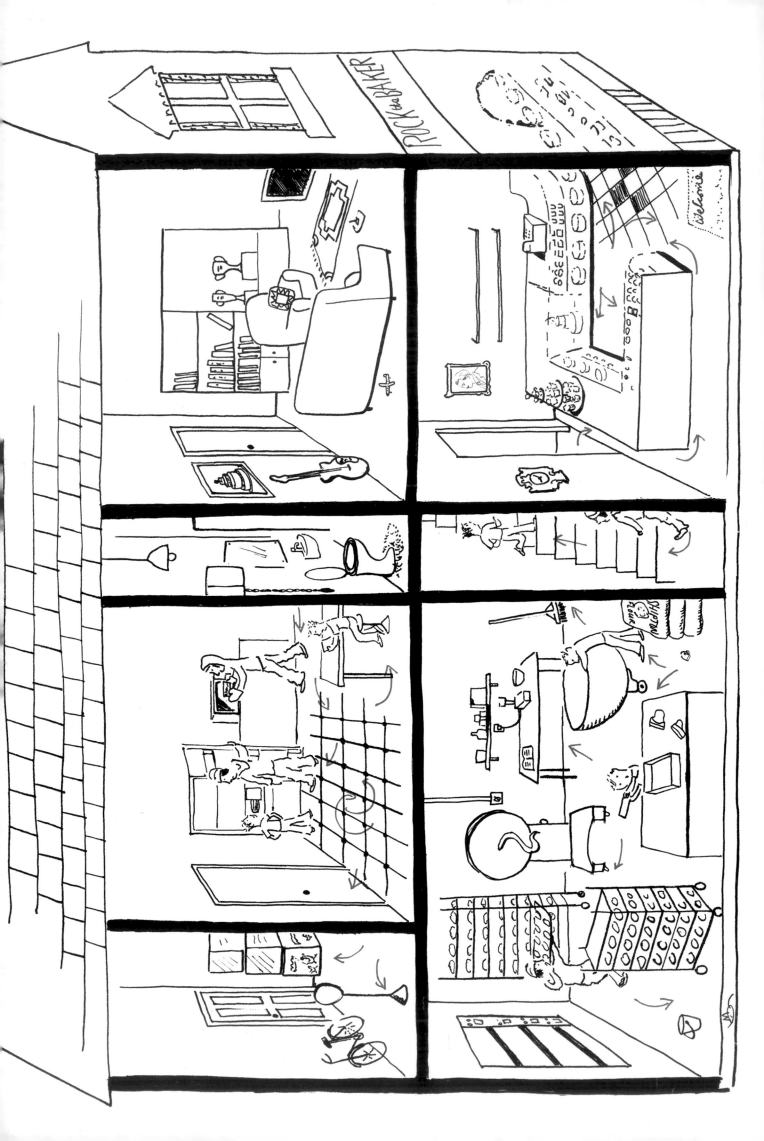

4

Kieran tried ringing Mr Rock on his mobile, but there was no answer.

They looked all around the bakery and in the shop, hoping to find a spare cake, but with no luck. So they went up to the flat hoping there might be something in the fridge.

There wasn't.

All they found was a chicken pie, which Mr Rock had left for their tea. It had a note on it saying, "Heat me."

Kieran was hungry so he put the pie in the microwave and turned the dial. But first, he pulled up his hood and put on an apron and a pair of oven gloves, in case a random microwave tried to zap him.

Ronny sat at the table looking at Mrs Mealman's letter.

"I must have dropped it," he said. "It's all my fault. Where am I going to get a Monster Cake now?"

"Simples," said Kieran. "We'll go to the supermarket, get a cake and put a photo of you on it!"

Ronny didn't laugh. "Can't you make a cake?"

"No, but I can make baked beans on toast," said Kieran thoughtfully, "although only if my mum opens the beans. And makes the toast. How about a Beans on Toast cake? Stick some candles on. I'd eat that. How old's this Alfie kid?"

Ronny looked at the letter. "Four," he said.

"Shazam!" said Kieran. "He's so small he'll never know the difference."

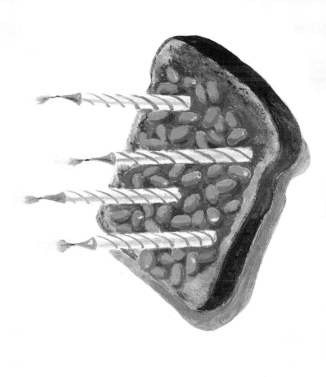

Ronny was not finding Kieran funny. "This is serious," he said. So Kieran suggested looking for a cake recipe. They looked through Mr Rock's cookery books but they were all written for professional bakers. *"Three kilos of butter, three kilos of sugar, four kilos of flour and 100 eggs,"* read Kieran. "Now that would be a Monster Cake!" He was keen to try it. But they only had a small box of eggs.

Then Ronny had a brain-wave. "What about your mum?" he said.

So they rang Tina. She gave them a recipe for a Victoria Sponge which, she said, made a very good birthday cake and only needed 200 grams each of butter, sugar and flour and four eggs. Then she told them how to cook a cake in the microwave. It seemed fairly simple.

"How come you can make a cake at Ronny's but you can't even manage to make a bowl of cornflakes at home?" asked his mum.

"KKKZZZZ . . . sorry, you're breaking up . . . KKKZZZZ. . . Mu . . . sig . . . gone . . . lu . . .," said Kieran and rang off.

5

"OK" said Ronny, once they had got some scales and weighed everything out. "I've watched my dad a million times and first you have to mix the butter and sugar together in a bowl really fast."

"Roger!" said Kieran and he attacked the bowl with a wooden spoon.

After twenty seconds he collapsed on the floor. "Black Hawk Down!" he croaked. "Arm ... malfunction ... need ... chicken ... pie..."

So Ronny took over the mixing for a bit.

Once they had both tasted it a few times they decided it was mixed enough. "Eggs go in next," said Ronny.

Kieran said he could crack eggs with one hand like a TV chef. But he was wrong. They fished out most of the egg shell with their fingers.

Finally they added the flour and the cake mix was ready.

The microwave went Ping! Kieran took the pie out and put the cake in.

While the cake was cooking, they ate the pie with lots of tomato sauce.

"What kind of Monster Cake are you going to make?" asked Kieran with his mouth full of sauce and pie. "One that looks like this?" He opened his mouth and made a horrible face.

"No," said Ronny, kicking him under the table. "The monster's going to look like Mr Bunt."

"YES!" shouted Kieran, joyfully thumping the table. "Yes, yes, yes. Yes, yes, yes, yes, YES!"

Kieran age 7

6 Mr Bunt was a HORRIBLE teacher who used to teach Kieran when he was little. Kieran said Mr Bunt personally hated kids. If anyone talked in class, he would make them stand on one leg on a chair. Worse, when he was on Lunch Duty he made children eat every single bit of their school dinners, specially the fatty bits.

Mr Bunt had bulgy eyes, hair like string, brown teeth and fat fingers like pink pork sausages. Worst of all, Kieran said he had awful fish breath which you could smell a mile off.

Mr Bunt had left teaching and gone off to be a slug farmer. Kieran said he felt sorry for the slugs. He wanted to set up "Slug Line" to help them cope.

A Monster Cake that looked like Mr Bunt would be perfect for Alfie Mealman.

Just then the microwave went *Ping!* again. But when Kieran took out the cake, Ronny's heart fell. It didn't look like the cakes his dad made. It looked weirdly pale and fat.

Ronny cut up half the cake to make the monster's head and body and the other half to make the arms and legs. Then he made some different coloured icings, but Kieran tickled him half way through and the colours got mixed up. A lot of the icing turned an ugly, sludgy green.

"That looks like snot," said Kieran happily.

Ronny used pink icing for Mr Bunt's face and snot-green for the body. He piped on some dirty, white, stringy hair. He made a monster mouth with brown almonds for teeth. Kieran rolled marzipan sausages for the porky fingers.

"Pretty good," said Kieran. "But the eyes need to be really mad and bulgy. Ooooh, I know ... ping-pong balls!" He got two out of his games bag and drew on two black pupils and some red veins.

"Ick!" said Ronny, because the eyes looked HORRIBLE. "What about the fishy breath?"

At the back of the fridge he found a half-eaten can of sardines. Perfect! They smeared fish-oil on the almond teeth.

cake for monster's body +  *cake for head* +  *cake for arms*

+ 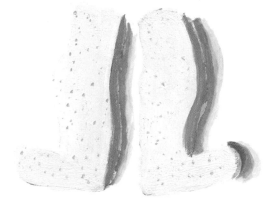 *cake for legs* +  *pink icing* +  *sludgy green icing*

+  *piped white icing* +  *brown almonds* +  *marzipan sausages*

+  *ping-pong balls* +  *fish-oil!!* =

TOO DISGUSTING TO BE SHOWN!

By now it was half past eight and Ronny's bedtime.
Ronny and Kieran propped Mrs Mealman's cake
letter up against the Monster Cake for Mr Rock to see.
Then they patted each other on the back and Ronny
went to bed. As he drifted off to sleep he imagined
little Alfie Mealman's happy face as, with tears in his
eyes, he thanked Ronny for THE BEST CAKE IN THE WORLD.

7 On Saturday morning, when Ronny woke up, his Monster Cake didn't seem such a great idea; particularly the fish-oil.

He jumped out of bed, got dressed quickly and went into the kitchen to look at it again. Perhaps he could wash the fish smell off.

BUT THE CAKE WAS GONE.

Ronny went downstairs to find his dad.

In the bakery it was the usual Saturday crush. Babies in pushchairs were clogging up the doorway. Builders were buying pies. Children were begging for doughnuts.

Tina, Kieran's mum, was behind the bread counter and waved at Ronny as he came in.

Mr Rock was at the cake counter, serving a man in a leather coat.

"Hi," said the man. "My name is Bran. I think you have a cake for my son."

Mr Rock produced a green cake box. "We certainly do. One Racing Car with its wheels on fire."

Mr Bran looked inside the box and smiled. "Cracking," he said. "Thank you."

Next was Mrs Yeast, holding the hand of a small fairy. They collected the Beautiful Butterfly cake. "Such craftsmanship," Ronny heard Mrs Yeast say.

Ronny's tummy started to squirm in a funny way.

Next in line was Mrs Bloomer who took away the Chocolate Train. Then Sophie Barm and her granny collected the Cat and Mice. "Isn't Mr Rock clever?" said Granny Barm as she went past. "Those little mice. You'd think they were real."

Ronny tried to catch his dad's eye by waving at him. He realized he had made a terrible mistake. His Monster Cake was not only going to spoil Alfie Mealman's birthday, it was also going to ruin his dad's reputation. Ronny waved frantically.

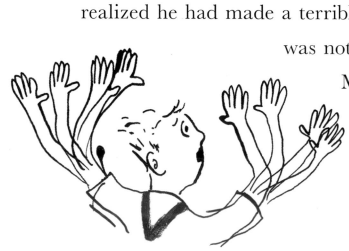

But Mr Rock was serving a woman and a very excited little boy who hopped about like a frog.

"Mrs Mealman," the woman announced.

The hopping boy began shouting, "It's my birfday and I'm getting a Monster Cakc! A Monster Cake, a Monster Cake! I'm getting a Monster Cake, a Monster Cake…"

"That's enough, Alfie," said his mum.

Ronny had reached a decision.

He would offer Alfie Mealman a lifetime supply of free doughnuts.

He would apologize to his dad.

Then he would run away to Antarctica and breed huskies.

But before Ronny could do any of those things, Mr Rock said to Alfie, "Happy Birthday, Alfie! Because this is such a special day we have made *two* Monster Cakes. You can choose which one you want."

And then Mr Rock glanced up at Ronny and winked.

Everyone in the shop was watching.

The kids all stopped drooling on the glass cabinets.

Tina looked over with interest.

Ronny held his breath.

MR ROCK OPENED THE FIRST BOX.

Inside was a cake Ronny had never seen before.
It was a big-eyed, toothy monster with blue icing fur.
It was perfect in every way.

"Oh, that's lovely," said Mrs Mealman. "Isn't he lovely, Alfie?"

Alfie said, "I like him. He's blue."

"Or," said Mr Rock, "you can have this Monster Cake."

MR ROCK OPENED THE SECOND BOX.

Everyone in the shop gave a kind of start. Tina said,

"OH NO!"

Alfie and his mother stared at the Mr Bunt Monster Cake.

Mrs Mealman's nose caught the faint pong of sardine.

"I think we'll take the other one," she began to say, but Alfie got in first.

"That's a n'orrible monster," declared the birthday boy. "I hate that monster! I want that monster!"

Other children crowded round to see.

"Yuck, that's gross," said one little girl.

"He ugly," said another.

"Cool!" said a boy wearing wheelies. "Mummy, I want that Monster Cake for my birthday."

Ronny couldn't believe his ears. But just as he was about to go over and give Alfie Mealman a mega-hug, a voice rang through the shop.

"Daddy, I wants to see the Monster Cake. Can I, Daddy? PWEASE!!!"

It was a small girl, sitting in her father's arms.

"Of course you can, Little Princess," said her daddy. And he put her down.

She marched over and stopped in front of Ronny and Alfie Mealman.

"Escuse me, pwease," she said sweetly.

Ronny and Alfie drew back to reveal The Cake.

Little Princess saw the angry pink face with the bulging eyes, the sticky out teeth and the porky fingers …

AND SHE SCREAMED.

"AAAAAARRRRRRGGGGGGHHHHHHHHHHH!"

And fainted.

This made all the other children scream too.

AAAAAAAAAAAAAAAAAAA
AARRRRRRRRGGGGGGH!

AAAAAAAAAAAAAAAAAAA
AARRRRRRRRRGGGGGGGH!

AAAAAAAAAAAAAAAAAAA
RRRRGGGGGH!

It was Monster Cake Meltdown!

Parents lost their children all over the bakery.

Tina found some hiding under the glass cabinet and
some in the flour sacks. One climbed up Mr Rock
and clamped onto his head like a monkey on a tree.

Little Princess was taken outside and revived.

Ronny calmed Alfie Mealman down by jamming a doughnut in his mouth. It's hard to cry and eat at the same time.

Ronny was on top of the world.

He had made the Monster Cake that Alfie wanted.

He had made The Cake that Alfie CHOSE!

And it had been scarily good.

As he stood there, watching Alfie Mealman chomping on doughnut, tears and snot, Ronny Rock had a funny feeling that maybe, just maybe, he could work magic like his dad.

Maybe,

one day

Rock the Baker

might

be

him.

Monster Quiz!

1. What colour are Ronny's trouser braces?
2. Where is the name "Rock the Baker" written on the shop?
3. Why is there a bucket by the shop door?
4. How much sense does Kieran have?
5. How many cakes does Ronny eat a year?
6. What is the name of the school lollipop man?
7. What is angelica?
8. Who ordered the Racing Car cake?
9. What is the name of this cake?
10. What did Mr Bunt do after being a teacher?
11. Who gave Ronny and Kieran the recipe for Victoria Sponge?
12. Whose jumper is this?
13. What dog does Ronny want to run away and breed?
14. What does Ronny want to be when he grows up?

The answers

1. Red
2. Above the window
3. To revive people
4. Less than a mealworm
5. 728
6. Stan Flan
7. Giant prehistoric parsley
8. Billy Bran
9. Toffee Tile
10. He became a slug farmer
11. Kieran's mum, Tina
12. Alfie Mealman's
13. Huskies
14. Rock the Baker, like his dad

Scores

All answers right –
you're a Master Baker!

Nine or more answers right –
you're an Able Baker!

Less than nine answers right –
you're a Junior Baker!

ting-a-ling

life is sweet